SUPERTATO

presents JACK AND THE BEANSTALK

Meet Sue and Paul:

Sue Hendra and Paul Linnet have been making books together since 2009 when they came up with *Barry the Fish with Fingers*, and since then they haven't stopped. If you've ever wondered which one does the writing and which does the illustrating, wonder no more . . . they both do both!

For Laura – the force is strong in this one.

SIMON & SCHUSTER

First published in Great Britain in 2022 by Simon & Schuster UK Ltd · 1st Floor, 222 Gray's Inn Road, London, WC1X 8HB
This edition published 2023 · Text and illustrations copyright © 2022 Sue Hendra and Paul Linnet
The right of Sue Hendra and Paul Linnet to be identified as the authors and illustrators of this work
has been asserted by them in accordance with the Copyright, Designs and Patents Act, 1988
A CIP catalogue record for this book is available from the British Library upon request · Printed in China
978-1-3985-1163-7 (HB) · 978-1-3985-1164-4 (PB) · 978-1-3985-1165-1 (eBook) · 978-1-3985-1232-0 (eAudio) · 10 9 8 7 6 5 4 3 2 1

SUPERTATO

presents JACK AND THE BEANSTALK

SUE HENDRA
PAUL LINNET

TICKETS

SIMON & SCHUSTER
London New York Sydney Toronto New Delhi

It's showtime in the supermarket
and the veggies are proud to present . . .
Jack and the Beanstalk.

"Once upon a time," Tomato began,
"there was a pea called Jack. He lived in
a tiny house with his mum and their
beloved cow, Daisy.

Jack didn't have a penny to his name, but he did have a good, kind heart."

So off Jack went to market to sell the cow.

On the way, he met a mysterious mango. "Hey, dude. Nice cow! How about you swap me your cow for these beans?"

"You want me to swap my cow for some **beans**?" said Jack.

"WHAT DO YOU THINK I AM?!
SOME KIND OF NITWIT?!"

"Easy, dude – these are magic beans!
They will bring you riches beyond
your wildest dreams!"

Hmmm . . . interesting,
thought Jack.

And he dashed home to
show his mum the new
beans. "Go on then,
BE MAGIC!"
he shouted at them.

But nothing happened.

"Why don't we put them on toast!" suggested Mum.

"NO!" spat Jack. "I'VE BEEN TRICKED! These beans aren't magic at all!" And with that, he flung them out of the window.

"WHERE THEY BELONG!"

But in the morning, when Jack woke up, he found something very strange outside.

"Maybe that nitwit Mango WAS telling the truth after all."

A huge beanstalk had grown and was stretching high up into the sky.

"Where are my riches then, Bean-cumber?" demanded Jack.

But it was too late. "HELP!" he cried as he began to fall.

Could this be the end for Jack?

"Don't panic!" called a voice from below.

In no time at all, they were through the clouds and could see a huge castle far off in the distance.

When they got to the door it was open, so in they went . . .

. . . and there on the table was a golden hen!

"I am the Golden Pineapple—
I mean Golden Hen and I lay
golden eggs! Just ONE of my
golden eggs will make you
rich beyond your
wildest dreams!"

"ONE?" snorted Jack.

"What do you mean
'just one'?!"

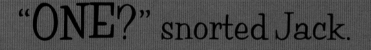

Then all of a sudden,
the ground started to shake,
and Jack and his mum heard
a loud, robotic voice.

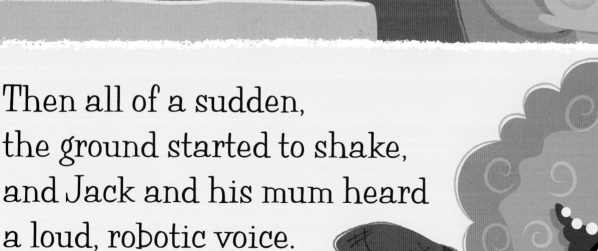

"WI-FI . . . FO . . . FUM, I . . . SMELL . . .
PEA, GONNA . . . EAT . . . ME . . . SOME!
BE . . . IT . . . ALIVE, OR . . . BE . . .
IT . . . DEAD, I'LL . . . GOBBLE . . .
ITS . . . LEGS . . . AND . . .
CRUNCH . . . ITS . . . HEAD!"

"Quick!" cried Jack.
"Let's hide in
this cupboard!"

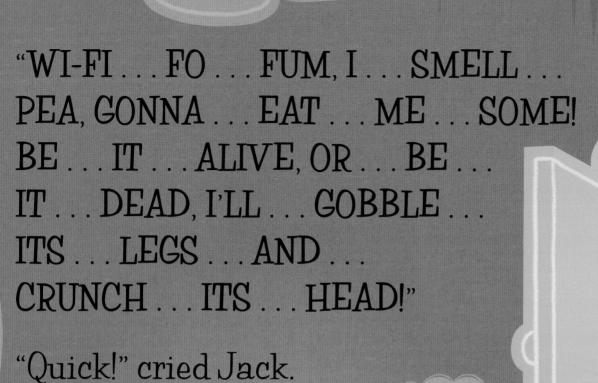

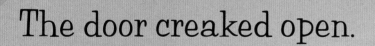

The door creaked open.

"WI-FI . . . FO . . . FUM,
I'M . . . GONNA . . . FIND . . . YOU . . .
HERE . . . I . . . COME!"

And with that, the giant melon-bot
flung open the cupboard.

"MUST . . . HAVE . . . PEA!" it said.

"HELP!" cried Jack and his mum, as they scrambled out of the cupboard and headed for the door.

"STOP . . . I'M . . . GOING . . . TO . . . EAT . . . YOU!" shouted the giant.

Jack and his mum dived through the clouds . . .

. . . and started to climb down the wobbly beanstalk.

But the giant was hot on their heels.

"WI-FI . . . FO . . . FUM . . . YOU . . . CAN'T . . . HIDE . . . YOU . . . CAN'T . . . RUN!"

"Quick!" shouted Jack. "We're almost there! Let's chop the beanstalk in half so that the giant can't catch us!"
"Good idea!" gasped Mum.

"WHAT"?!
Nobody's chopping
ME in half!" shrieked
the beanstalk.

And with that, it started
to run, bringing the
giant crashing towards
the ground.

"WI-FI . . . FO . . . FUM . . .
I . . . THINK . . . I'M . . .
GOING . . . TO . . .
BUMP . . .
MY . . .

... BUM."
said the giant,
in pieces on
the floor.

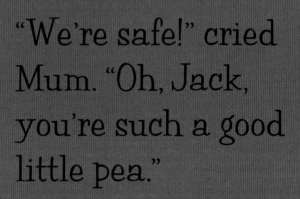

"We're safe!" cried
Mum. "Oh, Jack,
you're such a good
little pea."

"Oh no, I'm not!"
said Jack.

"Oh yes, you are!"
said his mum.

"Oh no, I'm NOT,"
said Jack.

Just then up popped the
Golden Hen. "I wonder what
happened to my golden
eggs?" said the Golden Hen.
"I've looked everywhere."

"Not everywhere,"
said Jack,
with a wink.

"We don't need riches,
do we?" said Jack's mum,
patting him lovingly
on the head.

CRUNCH!
CRUNCH!
CRUNCH!

"Not when we've
got each other."

"Ooo, it looks like you've got a bit of egg on your face!" chuckled the Golden Hen. "You didn't **really** think they were made of gold, did you?!"

THE END.

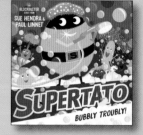

If you like

SUPERTATO

presents JACK AND THE BEANSTALK

you'll love these other

adventures from

SUE HENDRA &
PAUL LINNET

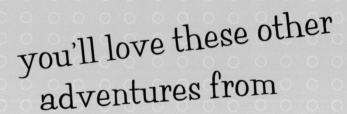

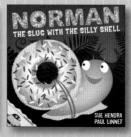